Race for the Mini-con Robots

Written by Michael Teitelbaum
Illustrated by Dreamwave Studios

Reader's Digest
Children's Books™

Pleasantville, New York • Montréal, Québec • Bath, United Kingdom

TRANSFORMERS™ Flip Book Fun
On the upper right-hand corner on the opposite page,
you'll see a TRANSFORMERS logo. Flip the pages
and watch the logo change!

CE
Published by Reader's Digest Children's Books
Reader's Digest Road, Pleasantville, NY U.S.A. 10570-7000
and Reader's Digest Children's Publishing Limited,
The Ice House, 124-126 Walcot Street, Bath UK BA1 5BG
Text copyright © 2003 Reader's Digest Children's Publishing, Inc.
Reader's Digest Children's Books is a trademark and Reader's Digest
is a registered trademark of The Reader's Digest Association, Inc.
Manufactured in China.
10 9 8 7 6 5 4 3 2 1

Contents

Prologue

Earth 2010

In a distant galaxy, far from Earth, the planet Cybertron was home to a race of intelligent, mechanical beings called Transformers. In addition, Cybertron itself was actually a living planet with its own consciousness and intelligence.

The Transformers possessed an amazing ability. They had the power to change their shape, reformatting themselves into machines or vehicles. When they completed this shape-shifting, the Transformers took on the characteristics and abilities of whatever they had morphed into.

For many years the Transformers lived in peace. They traveled into space, exploring new worlds and gaining knowledge. Aiding the Transformers in all their activities was a second race of small, but intelligent mechanical beings, called Mini-cons.

The Mini-cons attached themselves to the Transformers, increasing and enhancing their powers.

These useful beings were considered helpful tools that made the lives of Transformers easier.

Over time, however, the Transformers split into two groups. The first—who called themselves Autobots—believed in the peaceful way of life that had always existed on Cybertron.

A second group of Transformers, calling themselves Decepticons, craved power and domination. They viewed space travel as a way to gain control over other worlds, rather than to learn more about them.

The Decepticons also used Mini-cons to enhance their abilities. Unlike the Autobots, though, the Decepticons treated the Mini-cons cruelly, viewing them as slaves, rather than tools.

And so, a great war broke out—Autobots against Decepticons. Both armies tried to gain control over the Mini-cons, fighting for ownership of the small, yet useful machines. Each side hoped to manipulate the Mini-cons, realizing that they increased the power of any Transformer who combined with them.

Both sides believed that the Mini-cons held the key to victory. The war escalated, and the struggle for control of the Mini-cons almost destroyed Cybertron.

With both sides suffering great losses, a truce was finally called. It was decided to send the Mini-cons away from Cybertron so that they would never again be used as pawns in a war. All the Mini-cons on Cybertron were placed into an enormous spaceship and launched into space. The ship was sent through a warp gate, hurling it to a distant galaxy.

The ship was also equipped with a warp gate device which would instantly transport both the Autobots and the Decepticons to the ship if it was ever intercepted. This was done to guarantee that no one from another world would get hold of the powerful little machines.

During their journey, the Mini-cons' group intelligence grew. They gained the desire to be independent beings, free to choose their own destiny. Although neither the Autobots nor the Decepticons knew it, the Mini-cons were actually mechanical beings of high intelligence—in fact, another race of Transformers.

As the years passed, the Mini-cons were all but forgotten on Cybertron. They became the stuff of ancient myths and legends. Few Transformers believed that they ever really existed.

Eventually, war between the Autobots and the Decepticons broke out again on Cybertron. Even without the Mini-cons to fight over, the two sides resumed their age-old struggle for control of the planet.

Meanwhile, the Mini-cons emerged from the warp gate, arriving in the solar system that contained Earth. But the jump through the warp gate damaged their ship.

Reeling out of control, it slammed into Earth's moon, splitting in half.

Half of the ship crashed into the moon, scattering Mini-cons all over the lunar landscape. The other half of the ship crashed on Earth, scattering additional Mini-cons around the planet.

At this time in Earth's history, humans were primitive, living in caves, and had just discovered fire. Many years then passed on Earth, and the secret of the Mini-cons remained buried deep in a mountain cave.

In the year 2010, however, the Mini-cons were accidentally discovered by three kids, a 12-year-old boy named Rad, a 10-year-old boy named Carlos, and an 11-year old girl named Alexis. The three friends had been exploring the mountains near their home on the grounds of the Cosmo Scope Research Center and Interstellar Observatory in Colorado.

Exploring a mountain cave, they found the buried Mini-con ship that had crashed on Earth long ago. Awakening three Mini-cons, who had been dormant for many years, each of the three kids instantly bonded with one of the little robots. To the kids' utter amazement, when the Mini-cons spotted Rad's BMX bike, Carlos' skateboard, and Alexis' scooter, they instantly transformed into the shapes of those vehicles.

The Mini-con called High Wire bonded with Rad, and

changed into a BMX bike. The Mini-con called Grindor bonded with Carlos, and transformed into a skateboard. The Mini-con called Sureshock bonded with Alexis, and morphed into a motor scooter.

When the Mini-cons awoke, the warp gate device on their ship instantly transported the Autobots and the Decepticons to their location, bringing the ancient war from Cybertron to a new battlefield—planet Earth!

Megatron—the leader of the Decepticons—set up a base on the moon, using the section of the Mini-cons' ship that had crashed there as his fortress. From there, he planned to wage war against the Autobots. He began searching for Mini-cons of his own, armed with the knowledge that thousands of the valuable machines were scattered around the Earth and the moon.

On Earth, Rad, Carlos, and Alexis led Optimus Prime—the leader of the Autobots—to the Mini-cons' ship in the mountain cave. There, with the Mini-cons' help, Optimus Prime set up that section of the ship as his fortress in the coming war.

The three children promised to keep the Transformers' presence on Earth a secret. Then they headed home, hoping that they would meet Optimus Prime again.

They would, a lot sooner than they could have possibly imagined!

Chapter 1

Megatron's Mini-con Robot

The cold gray surface of the moon stretched endlessly in all directions. In the silent darkness of Earth's only natural satellite, a huge metal spaceship sprawled across the dusty ground. It was part of the spaceship that had carried the Mini-cons to Earth many years earlier. Now the giant structure was surrounded by an army of Decepticon soldiers.

The torn jagged edge of the ship—the spot where the vessel had split in half upon striking the moon—lay hidden in the ground. The remainder of the craft had been dug free by hundreds of Decepticons, and now served as the home base and fortress for the Decepticon invasion force. Robots crawled along the outside of the ship, completing repairs and wiring up systems controlling everything from communications, radar, and surveillance, to weapons and defensive shields.

Inside, Megatron paced anxiously, his bulky metal feet clanging against the steel mesh floor. The leader of

the Decepticons towered over the robots working busily all around him. He had no patience for the tedious task of connecting circuits and activating ancient systems.

"Faster!" Megatron bellowed. "All of you must work faster. I want this fortress ready. I want all systems operational. Now!"

The pace of work inside the fortress increased. Megatron walked briskly from one section of the ship to another, looking over the shoulders of the Decepticons who now worked furiously to meet his demands. Feeling he could do no more inside the ship, Megatron stepped through the hatch and strode out onto the powdery surface of the moon.

Looking up at the Earth, shining blue and white against the vastness of space, Megatron raised his enormous metallic arm. Reaching up, he spread his robotic fingers wide. Closing his fist, he blocked the Earth from his view. He pictured himself crushing the gleaming globe, wishing he could tear it from the black, star-filled sky.

"Earth!" Megatron spat out the name as if it were a curse. "Miserable little planet in this wretched galaxy. I would simply destroy it from here if it were not for the presence of the Mini-cons scattered throughout that pitiful little world."

Shaking his fist at the Earth, Megatron continued in

a loud, deep voice.

"And you, Optimus Prime, my old friend. Once again you challenge me for control of the Mini-cons, as you did long ago. But, do not worry. What was started four million years ago on Cybertron will be finished now on that tiny blue planet. I will defeat the Autobots, and take control of the Mini-cons. Combining their power with my own, I will then conquer the entire universe!"

Megatron's ranting was suddenly interrupted by a flash of metal from above. A Decepticon who had been adjusting a radar dish on the outside of the fortress lost control of a large tool he was using. The tool fell from the robot's hand, sailed over Megatron's head, and landed in the dusty lunar soil with a loud metallic clang.

"What is this?" Megatron screamed. He turned around and glared at the terrified robot clinging to the outside of the spaceship.

"My apologies, great Megatron," the robot said nervously. "The calibration device slipped from my—"

"Never mind that, Cyclonus!" Megatron yelled. "Get down here and help me."

"I don't understand, Megatron," Cyclonus said sheepishly. He climbed down and followed Megatron to the spot where the tool had landed. Cyclonus was proud to be part of Megatron's elite circle. He lived only to please his master.

"Didn't you hear the sound your tool made when it struck the ground?" Megatron asked. "That tool struck metal, not powdery moon dust. Something is buried right near our fortress."

Kneeling on the lunar surface, Megatron pushed the fallen tool aside, then brushed away the gray soil from the spot where it had struck. With Cyclonus assisting him, Megatron soon discovered the metallic edge of a rectangular panel. Working faster, the two Decepticons pulled the large panel from the ground.

Megatron's face lit up with excitement. He instantly recognized the object. "I have found a Mini-con panel!" he shouted. He drew himself up to his full height, towering over Cyclonus. Then he lifted the panel over his head. "It is mine!"

Lowering the panel, Megatron rested its base in the sandy soil. On the front of the panel was a drawing of a Mini-con robot.

"The time has come for you to awaken and serve me," he said, speaking directly to the image. Grabbing the panel on either side, Megatron sent electro-magnetic energy flowing into the large slab.

The panel began to glow brightly. Decepticons working all around the outside of the fortress turned toward the flashing of colors, then shielded their eyes from the blinding light. When the light faded, a Mini-con stood before Megatron, looking exactly like the picture on the panel.

"*Bubibibibibi!*" the little robot squeaked, as Megatron lifted it up to his shoulder. Although Megatron could not understand what the Mini-con was saying, the Decepticon leader felt an immediate and powerful bond with the tiny robot.

The Mini-con reached out with connectors which snapped into place perfectly, attaching to Megatron's shoulder. The two robots melded and transformed, with the Mini-con changing into the shape of a powerful machine gun.

"This Mini-con was destined for me!" Megatron shouted, feeling a surge of power rush though his robotic body. "It is a sign that we Decepticons will triumph!"

Megatron opened fire with his Mini-con machine gun, spraying bullets randomly in all directions. Puffs of dust sprang from the moon's surface where the bullets struck. Decepticons working up on the outside of the fortress tumbled to the ground. Others, including Cyclonus, ducked for cover behind the ship.

"HA! HA! HA!" Megatron laughed excitedly. "Behold the increased power of the mighty Megatron! The Autobots have their Mini-cons, and now I have mine! I will call it Leader-1, a fitting name for my Mini-con, don't you think?"

"Absolutely!" Cyclonus agreed, nervously edging back from behind the ship.

Leader-1 detached itself from Megatron's shoulder, changing from its machine gun form back to its original robot mode.

"Cyclonus!" Megatron shouted, his voice instantly turning serious again. "We have work to do. Starscream and Demolishor have been scanning images of all of Earth's vehicles. We must now join them in the fortress and choose our vehicle forms for the coming battle!"

Megatron hurried into the fortress, followed closely by Leader-1, then Cyclonus. Inside they joined two other Decepticons who stood before a giant viewscreen. On the screen, pictures of vehicles flashed quickly, ten at a time. The Decepticons viewed and instantly analyzed each group of vehicles as it appeared. Images of speeding cars, buses, commercial jet planes, tractors, bulldozers, and dump trucks filled the screen.

The Decepticons gasped in amazement at the next set of images. The screen was filled with photos of jet fighters, huge bombers, Army helicopters, giant missile-firing tanks, hand-held missile launchers, all-terrain armored vehicles, and a variety of military trucks. Each vehicle and weapon was captured in action unleashing its destructive force.

"I believe these are Earth's mightiest military

weapons," Demolishor explained. Like Cyclonus, Demolishor was one of Megatron's loyal lieutenants. He followed the Decepticon leader blindly, obeying his every command without question.

"Which vehicle do you choose, Megatron?" Starscream asked, offering the Decepticon leader the first choice. Starscream was the final member of Megatron's elite circle of command. He was a general in Megatron's army, and was second in power only to the Decepticon leader. Although he pretended to be loyal, Starscream believed that he should be the leader of the Decepticons. He was always looking for ways to weaken Megatron's rule and take the top spot.

"I choose that one!" Megatron announced pointing to a photo of a super tank with its guns blazing. Instantly, blueprints and technical specifications for the tank popped up next to the vehicle. Megatron scanned and downloaded the specs.

"Now it's your turn, my faithful general," Megatron said, looking right at Starscream. Megatron knew of Starscream's desire for power, yet his second-in-command was a fierce fighter and a valuable ally in the battle against the Autobots. Megatron did not trust Starscream, but, for the moment at least, he needed him.

"I choose that flying vehicle," Starscream said, pointing to a photo of a jet fighter soaring through the sky, firing on tanks below.

"I choose that flying vehicle," Cyclonus said, pointing to a picture of an Army helicopter hovering in the air as it unleashed an explosive barrage on a cluster of buildings.

"And I choose that one," Demolishor announced, pointing to a missile tank. Smaller than the super tank that Megatron had selected, Demolishor's choice featured a huge missile launcher, which in the photo was blasting a truck to smithereens.

As each of the Decepticons chose a vehicle form, its blueprints and technical specifications appeared on the viewscreen. After downloading this information, the Decepticons were now prepared for battle.

"Excellent!" Megatron roared, his voice echoing throughout the fortress. "You have chosen well, my friends. And now, it is time to pay a little visit to Optimus Prime and our Autobot friends on Earth!"

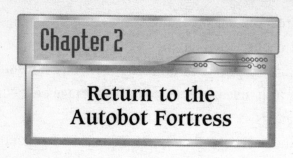

Chapter 2

Return to the Autobot Fortress

In the Cosmo Scope Research Center and Interstellar Observatory's school, three kids sat in different classrooms, each waiting for the school day to end, even more impatiently than usual.

Twelve-year-old Rad, ten-year-old Carlos, and eleven-year-old Alexis, all lived with their families on the grounds of the research center, and attended its school. They had recently had the adventure of a lifetime in the mountains near the observatory. The three friends had discovered an amazing race of mighty robot-warriors called Transformers. Now they could not wait to return to the mountain cave where they knew that Optimus Prime, leader of a group of Transformers known as Autobots, was hard at work setting up a fortress.

Rad, Carlos, and Alexis glanced at their watches every few seconds. They called themselves the Cosmo Kids, since they had gone to school at the Cosmo Center since kindergarten. Finally, the bell rang, releasing them for the day. They leaped from their seats and raced out of the school building.

Meeting in front of the school, the three friends smiled then banged their fists together in a gesture of friendship that had become their standard greeting. They had grown up together and were practically inseparable.

"You guys ready?" Rad asked, his blonde hair blowing in the breeze. Rad pulled his BMX bike from the bike rack and did his trademark handstand on the handlebars, then landed in a standing position with his feet on the pedals.

But this was no ordinary bike. Thin beams of light ran along the frame and handlebars, pulsing and shifting in color. The bike, in reality, was actually Rad's Mini-con High Wire.

"You bet I'm ready," Carlos replied, stepping onto his sleek skateboard, and running his hand through his dark, curly hair. The board itself was made of highly polished metal which gleamed in the afternoon sun. The skateboard's wheels glowed brightly. This was Grindor, Carlos' Mini-con. "I'm so ready I could hardly concentrate in science class."

"There's nothing unusual about that," Alexis said. She jumped onto her shimmering chrome scooter, which was covered with flashing lights. Her straight black hair bounced around her shoulders. "You couldn't concentrate in science class even before we met our Mini-cons and Optimus Prime."

"Could too!" Carlos shot back. "Just because you're the smartest kid in school, Alexis, doesn't mean that—"

Carlos was interrupted by a loud voice from behind.

"Hey, guys!" shouted a tall boy with close cropped brown hair. Next to him stood a shorter boy with copper-colored hair and a face full of freckles. "Fred and I were wondering where you got the radical new wheels," the taller boy said.

"Yeah," added Fred. "Billy and I want to know where they came from. I get all the BMX bike catalogs and extreme sports magazines. I've never seen those!"

Billy and Fred hadn't grown up at the research complex like Rad, Carlos, and Alexis, and they always felt like outsiders. They never quite fit in with the other kids at the complex. For a while, they hung out with Rad, Carlos, and Alexis, but their constant arguing and bossiness made the three old friends reluctant to spend time with the two newcomers.

Rad, Carlos, and Alexis looked at each other. They had made up a story to tell their parents about winning the new vehicles in an extreme riding competition. But they knew that story would never fly with these two.

"My dad got them for us," Rad said, breaking the uncomfortable silence. "You know he's got connections.

They're next year's models. They won't be in any catalogs or magazines until late this year."

"Yeah," agreed Carlos, impressed with Rad's ability to think on the spot. "Hey! We've got to go."

"See ya," Alexis added quickly, as the three friends took off.

"I don't believe them," Fred said.

"Me neither," said Billy. "Let's follow them and find out what they're really up to!"

****

"Breepitappapati!" Sureshock screeched, as Alexis raced along the road leading away from the complex and up toward the mountains.

"I think Sureshock said that was really a close one," Alexis translated.

Each of the three kids understood his or her own Mini-con, but not the others. The children had promised to keep the existence of the Mini-cons and the other Transformers a secret.

"Yeah," Carlos agreed. "The last guys we want finding out about our Mini-cons are Billy and Fred!"

"Hey!" yelled Rad as he zoomed along on High Wire. "There's the trail to the cave." Rad pointed to a narrow trail that led up to the highest peak of the mountains.

"I'm guessing that you three know the way," Alexis said to the Mini-cons.

"As a matter of fact, Alexis," Sureshock said, "my sensors are picking up readings from our ship."

The Mini-cons sped up the mountain trail. Riding on High Wire, Rad zoomed along, faster than he had ever ridden on any other BMX bike. "This is radical!" he shouted, standing up on the pedals, letting High Wire carry him along.

Crouching on Grindor, Carlos rode the skateboard Mini-con up the trail. Extending his arms, he pretended that he was flying, as Grindor did all the work. "Awesome!" Carlos exclaimed as he bounced along at high speed.

Sureshock provided the power, but let Alexis steer as the scooter Mini-con sped alongside the others. "Extreme!" Alexis yelled.

When the mountain trail reached the top of the first ridge, an even narrower path veered off to the left. One by one, the Mini-con vehicles made the sharp left turn, spraying dust and rocks from their tires and wheels.

The Mini-cons screeched to a stop at the top of the second path. The three friends were surprised to find that the opening, which had previously led into the mountain cave, was nowhere to be seen. In its place stood a door made from solid rock.

"It looks like Optimus Prime has been busy," Rad said, staring at the smooth face of the mountain. He could barely make out the edges of the door. Someone who didn't know that there once was an opening there would never have even suspected that this was a door.

Alexis stepped off Sureshock and ran her finger along the thin crack outlining the rock door.

"I guess he's prepared for another Decepticon attack," she said, hoping to find a way to open the huge door. "He couldn't just leave the entrance to his fortress wide open."

Carlos jumped off Grindor and joined Alexis in her search for a way into the cave. "I was hoping to see Optimus Prime again," he said, disappointed. "I don't suppose he put in a doorbell for visitors!"

"I believe we can help," High Wire said to Rad, rolling up to the door. "We are all tuned into the frequency of the equipment in the fortress, as it was formerly our ship." Lights on his handlebars flashed, and beeping, squeaking sounds chirped out of the BMX Mini-con.

"The controls that open the door are deep within the fortress," High Wire explained after a few seconds. "But I can operate them from here."

Rad, Carlos, and Alexis watched as High Wire sent a signal to a control panel inside the Autobot fortress. The

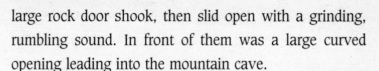

large rock door shook, then slid open with a grinding, rumbling sound. In front of them was a large curved opening leading into the mountain cave.

"Excellent!" said Rad, hopping back onto High Wire. "Let's move!"

Mounting their Mini-con vehicles, the three friends rolled into the cave. Each vehicle switched on a spotlight, illuminating the way.

"Awesome!" Carlos exclaimed as they zipped through the maze of tunnels leading down.

Arriving at the lowest level of the cave, the kids entered the huge metallic chamber which had once been the Mini-cons' ship. It was now set up to be the command center for the Autobots' defense of Earth against the coming Decepticon attack.

Long, thin lights ran along the high ceiling next to clusters of wires and pipes. The entire room was lined with computer consoles and control panels, which flashed and hummed with power.

"The Autobots have set up an impressive fortress," High Wire said, after he had finished running a scan of the equipment.

"Yeah," agreed Rad, looking around. "But where's Optimus Prime?"

Rad, Alexis, and Carlos searched every corner of the fortress, but there was no sign of the Autobot leader.

"I don't think he would just leave," Alexis said.

"Where would he go?" Carlos wondered. "It's not like he would just go catch a movie or grab a snack. And I think the sight of a twenty-foot-tall robot strolling around the mall would attract some attention."

"And he wanted his presence on Earth kept a secret," Rad added.

As the children pondered this mystery, Sureshock rolled over to a control panel. Extending a probe from the handlebars of her scooter form, the Mini-con plugged into the fortress' main computer.

"Each Transformer gives off an individual robotic signal," Sureshock explained to Alexis. "By searching for that signal, perhaps I can locate Optimus Prime."

A few seconds passed. Lights raced along Sureshock's handlebars and body. Then she withdrew her probe from the control panel.

"I have located Optimus Prime," she announced. "He is high in the mountains not far from here."

"Great!" exclaimed Alexis. "Let's go find him."

"In addition to his robotic signal, I have also picked up the signals of two other Transformers," Sureshock told Alexis.

"What does that mean?" asked Alexis.

"It means," Sureshock began, "that Optimus Prime is not alone."

Chapter 3

Transformation

Rad, Carlos, and Alexis streaked back through the tunnel leading from the Autobot fortress on their Mini-cons. "Maybe Megatron and the Decepticons came back!" Alexis said with concern.

"No," Sureshock assured her. "The robotic signals I received were not those of Megatron or his henchmen. I believe they belong to other Autobots."

"Sounds like Optimus Prime got some help," Rad noted after Alexis had translated Sureshock's comments for the others.

"Well, he can use all the help he can get," Carlos pointed out. "Those Decepticons were scary dudes!"

When the three friends emerged from the cave entrance, High Wire sent out a signal which closed the massive rock door behind them. As the giant door rumbled shut, the kids bounced along a mountain trail. Sureshock led the way, following the robotic signal given off by Optimus Prime.

Soon the friends came to the top of a rocky ridge. In

the distance, up at the top of the mountain, they spotted Optimus Prime. He was flanked on either side by two other Transformers, who were both smaller than the Autobot leader. All three Autobots peered out from the mountaintop, pointing urgently at something below.

****

Billy and Fred raced along the mountain trail on their BMX bikes. The last time they had followed the Cosmo Kids up into the mountains, the two boys squeezed past a pile of fallen rocks and entered the cave. But a rock slide that struck while they were in the cave frightened them so much that they fled and never spoke a word about their adventure to anyone. Still, they remained certain that Rad, Carlos, and Alexis had experienced something weird. And they were still determined to learn what it was.

"It's up there," Fred said, pointing to the narrow trail leading up to the cave.

"You don't have to tell me," Billy snapped at his friend. "I know."

Standing on their bike pedals for extra leverage, Billy and Fred pumped their way up the last leg of the trail. Reaching the cave entrance they stopped, then stared in stunned amazement.

"Where are all the rocks?" Fred asked in disbelief. "Last time we were here there was a big pile of rocks right there."

"I know," Billy shouted. "I was there, too, you know. I'm not stupid."

"And we were able to get into the cave through a tiny opening," Fred whined. "Where's the opening? There's nothing there now but a solid wall of rock!"

"And where did the famous Cosmo Kids go?" Billy asked, shaking his head, "Last time they went into that cave, I think. But there's no way to get in there now."

"Are we losing our minds?" Fred asked. "This is just too weird."

"I don't know," Billy replied, lifting the handlebars to his bike and turning it around. "Let's get out of here. This is stupid."

As Billy and Fred headed down the trail, Fred glanced back over his shoulder. Thinking now that he was really out of his mind, Fred could swear that he spotted four giant robots making their way up the side of the mountain.

Squeezing his hand brakes tightly, he skidded to a stop. "Billy!" he shouted, turning back around. "Look! Giant robots!"

"Yeah, right!" Billy cried, hitting his brakes and coasting to a stop. "You're real funny!"

"No, I swear, Billy!" Fred cried.

The two boys turned around quickly, but there was no sign of any robots. Overhead, a fighter jet and an Army helicopter roared past them.

"That's your idea of giant robots," Billy shouted. "A fighter and a chopper? You know there are military bases all around here. You're nuts. I'm going home."

Fred sighed and shook his head. *I know I saw four giant robots*, he thought. *Unless I really am nuts!* Pushing hard on his bike pedals, Fred hurried to catch up to Billy.

Below the sightlines of the two boys, hidden by the trees, two tanks—one a large super tank, and the other, a smaller one equipped with a missile launcher— rumbled up the mountain toward the Autobots' fortress.

****

Optimus Prime looked down from his vantage at the top of the mountain. Below, a highway ran through the dusty valley, splitting the dull brown soil with a ribbon of blacktop.

Two other Autobots stood beside him. The three Transformers were observing the highway, studying the various vehicles speeding along the road. Having the ability to transform into any vehicle they saw, the

Autobots were learning what they could about the vehicles of planet Earth.

"There!" shouted the Autobot to Optimus Prime's left, pointing to a sleek sports car tearing down the road at high speed. "That one's for me!"

"Very well, Hot Shot," Optimus Prime said in a deep even voice. "That vehicle does have the advantage of great speed. According to my scanner readings, it is moving at 110 miles per hour, faster than any other land-based vehicle we have seen so far."

"TRANSFORM!" Hot Shot shouted. Incorporating the elements he had seen on the sports car, Hot Shot folded his body in half, his arms touching the ground. Kneeling on his hands and knees, Hot Shot's body shimmered as it reformatted. Arms, legs, and eyes morphed into fenders, tires, and headlights, locking into place with a metallic snap. When the transformation was complete Hot Shot had assumed the form of a gleaming yellow sports car.

Gunning his engine, he peeled out, circling the mountaintop, kicking up rocks and spraying dirt onto Optimus Prime.

"That's enough!" Optimus Prime bellowed. "Save it for the Decepticons!"

Hot Shot screeched to a stop, then transformed back into his robot shape. He was young and full of spirit.

Sometimes he showed off a bit more than Optimus Prime would have liked. His flashy style upset the Autobot leader, but Hot Shot was loyal and a tough fighter in the war against the Decepticons.

BWEEE--O! BWEEE--O! BWEEE--O!

A piercing siren caught the Transformers' attention. Below on the road, a four-wheel-drive rescue vehicle—part ambulance, part fire truck, part armored car—raced to an emergency.

"I will take the form of that vehicle," said the Autobot to Optimus Prime's right, pointing to the four-wheel drive rescue vehicle.

"A good choice, Red Alert," Optimus Prime said.

"TRANSFORM!" shouted Red Alert. Taking on the appearance of the rescue vehicle, Red Alert reformatted himself. His body grew wide as extra metal plating wrapped all around him, locking itself into place. When the transformation was complete, Red Alert let out a loud siren and flashed his red emergency lights. Satisfied with his choice, he quickly morphed back into his robot form.

Red Alert was Optimus Prime's second in command. He was steady and determined. Unlike the more impulsive Hot Shot, Red Alert didn't take action without thinking his plan through first. He functioned as the Autobots' science officer, medic, and mechanic. He was Optimus Prime's right-hand man.

Optimus Prime stared down at the highway. Many vehicles roared past, but none felt right to him. Then he caught sight of a huge semi-tractor trailer. Its enormous cab contained a massive, powerful engine that hauled a long trailer. "A most impressive vehicle," Optimus Prime announced, pointing. "I choose that one!"

His attention was distracted by the sound of wheels crunching against the rocky ground. Turning, Optimus Prime spotted Rad, Alexis, and Carlos riding toward him on their Mini-cons.

"Hello," Optimus Prime said, when the three friends had skidded to a halt. "It is good to see you and your Mini-cons again."

Hot Shot and Red Alert stared in disbelief at High Wire, Grindor, and Sureshock.

"Mini-cons!" Hot Shot cried. "Then the legends are true!" Optimus Prime had told Hot Shot and Red Alert of the Mini-cons' arrival on Earth. He explained that their fortress was actually a piece of the Mini-con ship. But the two Autobots were still stunned to see Mini-cons with their own eyes for the first time.

"This is Hot Shot," Optimus Prime said, gesturing to the robot beside him. "And this is Red Alert. They are my teammates in the battle against the Decepticons."

The three Mini-cons beeped their greetings.

"Cool!" cried Carlos. "More awesome robots."

"They're called Autobots, Carlos," Alexis said.

"I know!" Carlos said quickly. "But they're still awesome robots!"

"How did you find us?" Optimus Prime asked.

"The Mini-cons were able to track your robotic signal from inside the fortress," Rad explained.

"I see," Optimus Prime said. "And why did you return to the fortress?"

"We want to help you in your battle against the Decepticons!" Carlos said proudly.

FOOM! FOOM! THOOM!

Deafening explosions rocked the mountain.

"Those explosions are coming from the fortress!" Red Alert cried.

"Decepticons!" Hot Shot snarled, spitting out the dreaded word.

"It appears, my friends," Optimus Prime said, turning and heading for the fortress, "that you will get you chance to help sooner than you thought!"

Chapter 4

The Decepticons Attack!

Rad, Carlos, and Alexis led the way on their Mini-con vehicles. The Autobots followed close behind. When they reached the cave entrance, the Transformers and the children were shocked to find a super tank blasting away at the stone door. Beside the super tank, a missile-launching tank also lobbed powerful explosives at the entryway. Above, an Army helicopter and a jet fighter fired machine-gun blasts at the entrance. The stone door remained in place, but it would not last much longer against the barrage unleashed by the transformed Decepticons.

Megatron caught sight of the three Mini-cons and stopped firing. "Halt your attack!" he ordered.

Instantly, the other three Decepticons stopped blasting the fortress.

"What we are seeking is right before us!" Megatron shouted as he transformed back into his robot mode.

Beside him, Demolishor morphed into his robot form.

Starscream and Cyclonus landed next to the other Decepticons and reformatted themselves back to their robot forms.

Megatron approached Rad, Carlos, and Alexis, glaring menacingly at their Mini-cons. "We will take those three Mini-cons now!" Megatron blustered, stepping toward them.

"Leave those kids alone, Megatron!" came a shout from behind the children. Optimus Prime stepped out from behind an outcropping. He was flanked by Hot Shot and Red Alert. "Or you'll have me to deal with," the Autobot leader threatened.

"Optimus Prime," Megatron bellowed. "So we meet again. I have no interest in these humans or in any other inhabitants of this pathetic little planet. I want those Mini-cons, and I will crush all who stand in my way!"

"You'll have to get past us first!" Hot Shot shouted, racing forward.

"Decepticons, TRANSFORM!" Megatron ordered.

The kids watched in amazement as Megatron reformatted into his vehicle mode. His massive body compacted and reshaped itself into a long gleaming metal box. His arms and legs folded under the box, snapping into place, morphing into thick treads. Rolling forward, he approached the advancing Autobots as an enormous super tank.

Demolishor transformed at the same time. His body also squared off to become a huge tank, but his legs became the treads, while his arms changed into two powerful missile launchers.

Cyclonus' body morphed into a large egg shape with a clear glass windshield. His legs changed into landing runners. His arms switched into helicopter blades which spun, faster and faster, lifting him into the air.

Starscream completed the evil quartet, transforming into a fighter jet. His body stretched into the shape of a giant bullet. His long arms widened into two triangular wings. Then his legs locked into place underneath him, forming landing gear and aerial machine guns. Then Starscream blasted off, joining Cyclonus in the sky.

These amazing transformations all took place within the space of a few seconds.

"They have assumed their vehicle modes!" Optimus Prime cried out.

"Then we Autobots must do the same!" Red Alert shouted. "TRANSFORM!"

Swiftly, Red Alert reformatted himself into a four-wheel-drive rescue vehicle. As it did before on the mountaintop, his body grew wider as extra metal plating wrapped all around him. His hands and feet morphed into thick, all-terrain wheels. Red Alert's siren screeched and his red emergency lights flashed.

Next to him, Hot Shot transformed into a gleaming yellow sports car. His body folded in half. His arms, legs, and eyes morphed into fenders, tires, and headlights.

"My turn!" shouted Optimus Prime as the Decepticons rushed toward them. Although he had not had a chance to practice the transformation when he first observed the semi-tractor trailer on the highway, Optimus Prime was very experienced in reformatting himself into any vehicle he observed. "TRANSFORM!"

Optimus Prime's head expanded, squaring off into the shape of an enormous tractor cab. His neck stretched, forming the coupling device which attached the cab to the long trailer behind it. His body elongated, forming the trailer. Then his hands and feet divided again and again until they had morphed into the giant truck's eighteen wheels. His arms and legs fused together, forming the large rectangular container box that rested on the trailer portion of the vehicle.

"I feel great power in this form!" Optimus Prime shouted as he revved his huge engine.

"I suggest we find cover," High Wire said to Rad, who translated for the others. "Perhaps we should slip into the fortress until the fight is over."

"No way!" Carlos exclaimed, when Grindor told him about High Wire's idea. "I don't want to miss this outrageous battle."

"Then maybe we should try to find a hiding place," Alexis suggested.

"Excellent idea, Alexis," Sureshock said. Alexis led the others to a thick cluster of nearby trees, where they nestled in to watch the coming clash.

BAASSHHH!

Optimus Prime slammed into Megatron's tank form, sending the Decepticon leader tumbling out of control.

Seeing this, Demolishor fired a missile from the launcher atop his tank. Red Alert reacted quickly, speeding to Optimus Prime's side. He deflected the missile with his armor-plating, sending it veering off into the woods where it exploded harmlessly.

"Thanks, Red Alert," yelled Optimus Prime.

"Anytime, boss," replied Red Alert.

"Look out above!" shouted Hot Shot, his sports car skidding to a stop beside his teammates. "Incoming!"

Cyclonus and Starscream swooped down from the sky, their machine guns blazing. Hot Shot peeled out, tires squealing to avoid the aerial blasts. Red Alert circled around Optimus Prime deflecting as many bullets as he could, but he could not stop them all.

PING! PING! ZING!

Bullets struck Optimus Prime in his cab and container. "I can't stop the bullets in this form," the Autobot leader cried. "I must transform again, this time into Super Optimus Prime!"

As the leader of the Autobots, Optimus Prime had a special power. Only his closest teammates knew about it. He had the ability to transform into an even bigger robot by incorporating his vehicle form into his huge body.

Optimus Prime began to grow. The ground shook fiercely, and the thunderous clanging of metal on metal filled the air. Bigger and bigger he grew, sprouting enormous arms and legs, his body expanding in height and width. Finally, the remarkable transformation was complete. The semi-tractor trailer truck, which moments before had seemed so huge, was now just a section of the giant robot, serving as one of Optimus Prime's feet.

From his hiding place among the nearby trees, Carlos stared open-mouthed at the towering form of Super Optimus Prime.

"Wow!" he cried, pointing at the gigantic Autobot leader. "Now that's what I call one awesome robot!"

Catching sight of Super Optimus Prime, Cyclonus and Starscream stopped their attack and flew back toward Megatron. The Decepticon leader was stuck on his side, unable to right himself. Struggling clumsily in their vehicle forms, the two Decepticons finally managed to flip Megatron over onto his tank treads.

Optimus Prime strode toward Megatron, taking long steps that shook the mountains. "You will leave now,

Megatron!" he shouted, moving closer to the super tank.

"Stop him!" Megatron ordered his teammates.

Cyclonus and Starscream took to the air again, circling around Super Optimus Prime. The giant Autobot swatted at the helicopter and fighter jet as if they were insects buzzing around his head. The two flying Decepticons fired their machine guns, but the bullets bounced off Optimus Prime in his super robot form. They were more of an annoyance than a real threat.

Hot Shot and Red Alert raced toward Megatron and Demolishor, hoping to distract the two Decepticon tanks. But the tanks ignored them, rumbling forward toward Super Optimus Prime.

"Optimus Prime has grown even more powerful!" Megatron said to Demolishor. "But so can I!"

Megatron pulled out Leader-1, the Mini-con he had found on the moon, and attached it to the top of his tank form. Connecters shot out from Leader-1, snapping into place on Megatron as if they had been designed exactly for just that purpose.

"This is the secret power of Megatron!" he shouted. "The power to control not only Earth and Cybertron, but the entire universe!"

From their hiding place, Rad, Carlos, and Alexis, along with High Wire, Grindor, and Sureshock watched as Megatron and his Mini-con both transformed.

Megatron doubled in size, and Leader-1 morphed from a small machine gun into a giant cannon, which now stuck out from the top of the tank.

"Wow!" exclaimed Carlos. "The Mini-cons really do increase the power of the Transformers."

"That is correct, Carlos," Grindor said. "That is why both the Autobots and the Decepticons so desperately want to capture us and our fellow Mini-cons."

"Behold the power of the Mini-cons!" Megatron declared. Aiming right at Super Optimus Prime, he fired Leader-1 at his foe.

THOOM!

A powerful blast exploded from the muzzle of Leader-1's cannon, flying wildly out of control. The recoil from the shot was so strong, it caught even Megatron off-guard. He realized instantly that this was by far the most powerful weapon he had ever commanded in all his years of battling the Autobots.

The Decepticon leader toppled over backwards from the recoil from the cannon blast. Megatron knew he would have to practice in order to gain control of the weapon, but he was still thrilled by its incredible power.

"HA! HA! HA! HA!" Megatron cackled. "The power of the Mini-cons is mine!"

The energy from the blast also knocked Super Optimus Prime off his feet, even though the shell Leader-

1 had fired missed him by a wide margin. He crashed to the ground with a clanging thud, stunned by the force of the blast. Nearby, Red Alert spun out of control, rotating at dizzying speed.

Shock waves from the explosion also slammed into Cyclonus and Starscream, forcing them to crash land near their fallen leader. Dazed, they tried to regroup, as Megatron attempted to right himself.

The huge shell shot from Leader-1 completely missed its target—Super Optimus Prime. Instead, it slammed into the mountain behind the giant Autobot, exploding with a deafening roar.

When the dust from the explosion cleared, a terrifying sound could be heard. The deep rumble started slowly, then built in intensity.

Looking up from his hiding place, Rad spotted a rock slide tumbling down the mountain face, heading right for him, his friends, and their Mini-cons.

Chapter 5

Mini-con Robots to the Rescue

Massive boulders and big chunks of jagged rock roared down the mountainside, stirring up a huge dust cloud.

"Rock slide!" Rad shouted. "We'll never get away in time! Even on our Mini-cons!"

Suddenly, a yellow blur came streaking toward them and skidded to a stop. "Anybody need a ride?" asked Hot Shot in his gleaming yellow sports car form. He revved the powerful engine, then popped opened his doors. "Hop in!"

Rad, Carlos, and Alexis leaped into the car, and their three Mini-cons quickly attached themselves securely to the sports car's rear bumper. Hot Shot peeled out, streaking away from the mountain, just as the rock slide hit—right in the spot where they had been standing.

CRASH!

Piles of rocks struck the ground with a thunderous crash. The sound grew louder, then slowly faded as the last pebbles bounced down, leaving a huge cloud of dust and an eerie silence.

Hot Shot maintained his speed, trying to keep a safe distance from the mountain.

"Hey!" shouted Carlos as the three friends tumbled around in the small car. "It's crowded in here." Rad's elbow was stuck in Carlos' ear, and Alexis kept poking him in the ribs.

"Well, what do you expect?" Alexis said, shoving Carlos' sneaker away from her nose. "Sports cars only have two seats!"

"Would you rather we left you back there?" Rad asked, pointing to the scene of destruction caused by the rock slide.

Hot Shot slammed on his brakes, tossing the kids into a new jumble of arms and legs. "I've got to head back to help Optimus Prime," he said.

"Well, what are you waiting for?" asked Rad. "We're with you!"

Racing back to the battle, Hot Shot sped around the edge of the newly formed pile of boulders. As they zoomed past, Alexis gasped.

"Look!" she cried, pointing to something sticking out from the pile of rocks. "Hot Shot, stop! Please!"

Hot Shot hit his brakes, spun around, then skidded to a stop. "What?" he asked. Then he caught sight of the objects Alexis had seen. "What are those things?"

Alexis quickly climbed from the sports car and scrambled up the rock pile. There, sticking out from the rubble, were four Mini-con panels. Alexis recognized them immediately. They were very similar to the panels from which her own Mini-con and the Mini-cons of her friends had emerged.

"Mini-con panels!" Alexis shouted. "Four of them."

Rushing from Hot Shot's seats, Carlos and Rad joined Alexis on the rock pile. Each child lifted one Mini-con panel from the rocks. Hot Shot bounced up the bumpy pile, changed his front tires back into robotic hands, and snatched the last panel.

Instantly the panel began glowing. Hot Shot sensed a strong connection with the shimmering rectangle in his mechanical hands. The panel began to transform, stretching, growing long and thin, then reformatting into a jagged shape resembling a lightning bolt. The lightning bolt Mini-con combined with Hot Shot, attaching to the front of the car, like a giant hood ornament.

As Hot Shot gunned his engine, his Mini-con crackled with electric energy. A jagged bolt of electricity shot from the Mini-con, crackling and sizzling around the base of the rock pile.

"All right!" cried Hot Shot. "Now I understand the increased power Mini-cons can give Transformers. I'll call him Jolt. He packs quite a wallop!"

Red Alert, recovered from the explosion, zoomed up alongside Hot Shot.

"So you've found a Mini-con!" he said, slightly envious of his teammate.

Before Hot Shot could respond, the Mini-con panel that Carlos was holding started to glow. The radiant panel flew out of Carlos' hands and floated through the air toward Red Alert. Red Alert immediately felt a strong bond with the tiny machine. The Mini-con then morphed into a giant mechanical arm. The huge arm combined with Red Alert, who suddenly felt increased power surging through his body.

Red Alert reached out with his giant Mini-con arm, gently grabbing Hot Shot and lifting him into the air. "This power is incredible!" he cried, thrilled with his new partner. "I will call my Mini-con Longarm!"

"That's what I call strong!" said Hot Shot, dangling ten feet off the ground. "Now would you mind putting me down, please?"

"You hold the other two Mini-cons until the battle is over," Red Alert said to Rad and Alexis, who clutched the panels tightly. "I'm sure Optimus Prime will want to see them. Right now, we've got to go back and help him finish off those Decepticons!"

"You bet!" Rad cried.

"You can count on us!" Alexis added.

"Hey, that's not fair!" Carlos whined. "Red Alert took my panel!"

Alexis rolled her eyes. "It wasn't your panel," she said. "Didn't you see it was destined for Red Alert, just like Grindor was destined for you?"

"Oh yeah," Carlos said, smiling. Then he hopped onto Grindor and skateboarded to a hiding spot among the fallen rocks, followed closely by Rad on High Wire and Alexis on Sureshock.

Hot Shot and Red Alert sped back to the spot where Optimus Prime had fallen. As the giant Autobot leader struggled to his feet, he noticed the new Mini-con attachments on his teammates. "So you have found Mini-cons!" he shouted, amazed at their good luck.

"Yes," replied Hot Shot, charging up Jolt. "And the increase in power is huge."

A short distance away, Demolishor and Starscream morphed back into their robot forms. They found it much easier to help flip Megatron back onto his tank treads, using their robotic arms.

"Don't worry about me!" Megatron muttered, when he was once again upright. "Go finish off Optimus Prime!" he commanded.

"Yes, Megatron," Demolishor replied quickly, changing back into his missile tank vehicle mode.

"Of course," Starscream said, secretly hoping that

Optimus Prime would destroy Megatron, which would leave him in charge of the Decepticons.

Starscream reformatted back into his jet fighter mode and took off, tearing through the sky, with Demolishor rolling along on the ground beneath him. Cyclonus, who had remained in his helicopter form, joined the others. The three Decepticons rushed toward Hot Shot, Red Alert, and Optimus Prime.

Starscream and Cyclonus swooped down toward the huge robotic form of Optimus Prime. "You will not succeed this day, Decepticons!" the Autobot leader shouted, swatting at the helicopter and fighter jet with his enormous robotic hands.

The two flying Decepticon vehicles went plunging to the ground, spinning out of control.

Demolishor aimed the missile launcher on the top of his tank right at Optimus Prime. But just as he fired, Red Alert reached out and grabbed the Decepticon missile tank with Longarm. He lifted Demolishor into the air, sending his missile flying off target. It exploded harmlessly in the canyon beyond.

"Guess what, Demolishor," Hot Shot shouted. "Red Alert here isn't the only one with a brand new Mini-con!" He fired a jagged bolt of electrical energy from Jolt. The searing power charge surrounded Demolishor, shorting out his circuits.

"Now, fly like your teammates!" said Red Alert, hurling the defeated missile tank through the air with his powerful Mini-con arm.

Demolishor tumbled through the air, finally crashing on the ground right next to Megatron.

"You incompetent fools!" Megatron screamed. "I will destroy Super Optimus Prime myself!"

Megatron rumbled forward, swiveling his Mini-con cannon toward Super Optimus Prime. The Autobot leader charged forward, reaching Megatron in two enormous strides of his huge legs.

"Your henchmen could not defeat me, Megatron!" Optimus Prime shouted, "and neither will you!" Optimus Prime grabbed Megatron in his massive mechanical hand and lifted him off the ground.

"Wrong again, Optimus Prime!" Megatron shouted, activating the firing mechanism on Leader-1.

Using his great strength, Optimus Prime grabbed the long cannon section of Leader-1 and bent it skyward, just as Megatron fired.

THOOM!

Once again a powerful blast exploded from the muzzle of Megatron's Mini-con. But this time the explosive shell soared high into the air, detonating harmlessly in a display of smoke and orange flame, like a giant fireworks show.

The force of the shot propelled Megatron backwards, throwing him free of Optimus Prime's grasp. Slamming hard into the ground, Megatron called out to his troops.

"We are outmatched today, Decepticons!" he cried. "Retreat! Retreat!"

Megatron opened a warp gate and prepared to make his escape. "Next time, Optimus Prime, the outcome will be different!" Then he vanished into the warp gate, disappearing in a blinding flash.

Nearby, Demolishor and Starscream activated their own warp gates. Two brilliant bursts of light flooded the mountainside. When the lights faded, the two Decepticons were gone.

Only Cyclonus remained. The determined Decepticon, in his helicopter form, swooped down toward the Autobots, who had all gathered around Optimus Prime.

"Does he really think he can take us all on?" Hot Shot asked.

"If so, he's about to get a rude awakening," Optimus Prime promised.

But at the last second, Cyclonus veered away from the Autobots, speeding toward the three children who crouched among the nearby trees.

Alexis looked up from her hiding spot. "The others have all gone," she said nervously. "But that helicopter

Decepticon is headed this way!"

"He's after us!" Carlos cried out in fear.

"I don't think so," Rad said calmly. "He's overhead, staying above us."

"Then what does he want?' Carlos asked anxiously.

Without warning, Cyclonus reformatted the two landing runners on the bottom of his helicopter body, changing them back into his robotic arms. Reaching down swiftly, Cyclonus snatched the two Mini-cons from Alexis and Rad, one in each hand, and pulled them up into his body.

"Thanks!" he said wickedly. *This little maneuver should place me in excellent favor with Megatron*, he thought. Then he suddenly vanished in a bright burst, slipping through a warp gate.

"They're gone!" Carlos shouted, staring up into the empty sky. "That Decepticon has stolen the Mini-cons!"

Chapter 6

Power Play

The barren darkness of the moon's surface was suddenly shattered by a blazing flash of light. A warp gate opened, then closed just as quickly. Megatron appeared on the cold gray landscape with Leader-1 still attached. Separating from Megatron, Leader-1 reformatted into his robot mode. Then Megatron did the same. All around them, Decepticons continued working busily on their fortress.

A warp gate flashed again and Demolishor appeared. Another flash and Starscream stood before them. They both quickly morphed into their robot forms, as well.

"Another defeat, Megatron," Starscream said mockingly. He never passed up an opportunity to point out his leader's failures.

"And I suppose you played no part in this humiliation," Megatron shot back, his anger growing.

"We *will* be victorious next time, Megatron," Demolishor said quickly.

"Are you his lieutenant or his pet, Demolishor?"

Starscream said accusingly.

"I will show you what I am!" Demolishor roared, rushing at Starscream.

The two Decepticons locked arms, wrestling with each other and exchanging blows until they tumbled to the ground.

"Stop this at once!" Megatron shouted, but the fighting continued.

"TRANSFORM!" Demolishor shouted, shoving Starscream away. Within seconds he had reformatted himself into his missile tank mode. He fired a missile right at Starscream.

"TRANSFORM!" Starscream called out, morphing into his fighter jet mode. Blasting into the sky, Demolishor's missile whizzed past him, exploding in a nearby crater.

"ENOUGH!" Megatron bellowed. "There is nothing to be gained by fighting among ourselves!" Lashing out with his powerful robotic hand, Megatron grabbed Demolishor's missile launcher and turned it away from Starscream. He then reached up with his other hand and swatted the fighter jet from the sky, sending it crashing into the soft, powdery surface of the moon.

A brilliant flash suddenly caught the attention of all three Decepticons. Cyclonus suddenly emerged from a warp gate, triumphantly holding two Mini-con panels

over his head.

"Some souvenirs of our visit to Earth, Megatron," Cyclonus said proudly.

Demolishor and Starscream morphed back into their robot forms.

Megatron smiled. "Nice work, Cyclonus," he said, taking the two panels. "It is nice to see that someone around here speaks with action rather than taunts and empty threats. It appears that our battle on Earth was not without a victory."

Starscream glared at Cyclonus. He knew that Cyclonus would do anything to gain favor with Megatron, and now he had captured a glorious prize. His own dreams of replacing Megatron would have to wait a little longer. In the meantime, he would claim his right to one of the Mini-cons and increase his power.

"Yes, nice work, Cyclonus," Starscream said, barely able to spit out the words. "And now I will take the Mini-cons." He reached out toward Cyclonus.

"No!" shouted Megatron, shoving Starscream's hand away. "Since Cyclonus captured the Mini-cons, one shall be his."

"Thank you, Megatron," Cyclonus said. He held the two Mini-cons out in front of him, one in each hand. The panel in his right hand began glowing, the image of a robot shining from its smooth metallic front. "I choose this one!" He then handed the other panel to Megatron

The glowing slab morphed into a tiny robot that looked like the image that had been on the panel. The robot beeped and chirped happily.

"He is called Crumplezone," Cyclonus reported. "And I shall soon learn how he can increase my power!"

"Very well," Starscream said with a sigh. "Then I will have the other."

"I choose to give this second Mini-con to Demolishor," Megatron said, seizing the opportunity to keep Starscream's power in check.

"What?" Starscream blustered. "But I am second in command here!"

"Exactly," Megatron said, not even trying to disguise his contempt. "And therefore you should be skilled and powerful enough to find your own Mini-con!"

"Thank you for this great honor, Megatron," Demolishor said, taking the second panel from his leader's hand. He smiled triumphantly at Starscream.

Starscream looked away, fuming. He would indeed find his own Mini-con, and when he did, he would deal with Demolishor and with Megatron.

The Mini-con panel in Demolishor's hands began to glow, then it transformed into its robot mode. It hummed and buzzed.

"This one is called Blackout," Demolishor explained.

"And together we will work to crush the Autobots and gain control of Earth!"

"Hear me well, all Decepticons!" Megatron shouted in a deep, booming voice. All work on the fortress suddenly stopped. Every Decepticon on the moon base turned to face their leader. "The acquisition of these two new Mini-cons is a great victory for us. But there are still Mini-cons scattered all over the moon and the Earth. We must not rest until we have captured every one!"

Then Megatron strode into his fortress, satisfied that very soon he and the Decepticons would once again face Optimus Prime and the Autobots in the continuing battle for the Mini-cons.

Epilogue

A Circle of Friendship

At the Autobot fortress on Earth, Alexis stared at the spot where, seconds earlier, Cyclonus had vanished with the two Mini-con panels.

"I can't believe we let the Decepticons get those Mini-cons," she said sadly.

"Yeah," Rad added. "We should have stopped him!"

"There was nothing you could have done," Optimus Prime said softly. He and the other Autobots had returned to their robot forms and now stood before the entrance to the fortress. "Cyclonus moved swiftly and staged a surprise attack. Now they have two Mini-cons, and we have two." He gestured to Hot Shot and Red Alert who stood beside their Mini-cons, also in their robot modes.

"And don't forget about Grindor, High Wire, and Sureshock!" Carlos added.

"*Breeeebibipi!*" Grindor beeped.

"You're welcome," Carlos replied.

Alexis looked up at Optimus Prime. "I'm sorry we

woke up the Mini-cons and re-started your war," she said, shaking her head. "I feel like we're somehow responsible for all this."

Optimus Prime knelt down beside Alexis and placed his huge metal hand gently onto her shoulder. "This war has been raging for million of years," he explained. "What happened today was one small battle in the conflict. We are the ones who programmed the Mini-cons long ago to activate the warp gate and bring us to them if they were discovered. It was inevitable that someone would find them sooner or later."

He looked right into Alexis' eyes. "I am glad that trustworthy humans like you and Rad and Carlos found them, rather than someone else."

The three Mini-cons beeped their agreement.

"You were destined to find each other," Optimus Prime continued, indicating the three children and their Mini-cons. "You belong together."

"We want to help you," Alexis announced boldly, placing her hands on her hips. "In your war with the Decepticons."

"Yeah," agreed Rad. "We want to help you defeat the Decepticons."

The two friends looked at Carlos. He appeared to be a bit nervous. "Well, if you two are in," he said, swallowing hard and hiding his fear, "then you can count me in, too!"

Optimus Prime shook his massive metal head. "I hesitate to involve you," he said, concern evident in his voice. "As you have seen, this is a dangerous business."

"But we want to help," Alexis replied, "since we're the ones who brought this war to Earth. And our Mini-cons want to help, too, don't you?"

Grindor, High Wire, and Sureshock chirped their agreement in unison.

Optimus Prime laughed. "Very well," he said. "You may assist us. If you are careful."

"Oh, we will be," Carlos said bravely. "And next time that Cyclonus won't get away so easily!"

Rad, Carlos, and Alexis gently banged their fists together. Seeing this, Optimus Prime, Hot Shot, and Red Alert reached out with their huge robot fists and joined them in a circle of friendship.